Dear Parents and Educators,

Welcome to Penguin Young Readers! As parents and educators, you know that each child develops at his or her own pace—in terms of speech, critical thinking, and, of course, reading. Penguin Young Readers recognizes this fact. As a result, each Penguin Young Readers book is assigned a traditional easy-to-read level (1–4) as well as a Guided Reading Level (A–P). Both of these systems will help you choose the right book for your child. Please refer to the back of each book for specific leveling information. Penguin Young Readers features esteemed authors and illustrators, stories about favorite characters, fascinating nonfiction, and more!

Strawberry Shortcake™
The Butterfly Parade

LEVEL **2**

GUIDED READING LEVEL **H**

This book is perfect for a **Progressing Reader** who:
- can figure out unknown words by using picture and context clues;
- can recognize beginning, middle, and ending sounds;
- can make and confirm predictions about what will happen in the text; and
- can distinguish between fiction and nonfiction.

Here are some **activities** you can do during and after reading this book:
- Make Connections: In this book, Strawberry Shortcake and her friends have a parade to celebrate spring. Have you ever been to a parade? Draw a picture and tell a story about what you were celebrating.
- Picture Clues: Use the pictures to tell the story. Have the child go through the book, retelling the story just by looking at the pictures.

Remember, sharing the love of reading with a child is the best gift you can give!

—Bonnie Bader, EdM
  Penguin Young Readers program

*Penguin Young Readers are leveled by independent reviewers applying the standards developed by Irene Fountas and Gay Su Pinnell in *Matching Books to Readers: Using Leveled Books in Guided Reading*, Heinemann, 1999.

PENGUIN YOUNG READERS
An Imprint of Penguin Random House LLC

Strawberry Shortcake™ & © 2016 Shortcake IP Holdings LLC.
Used under license by Penguin Young Readers Group. All rights reserved.
Published by Penguin Young Readers, an imprint of
Penguin Random House LLC, 345 Hudson Street, New York, New York 10014.
Manufactured in China.

ISBN 978-0-448-49008-3   10 9 8 7 6 5 4 3 2 1

PENGUIN YOUNG READERS

LEVEL

2

PROGRESSING
READER

Strawberry Shortcake

The
Butterfly Parade

by Mickie Matheis
illustrated by Laura Thomas

Penguin Young Readers
An Imprint of Penguin Random House

Spring has arrived in

Berry Bitty City.

Strawberry Shortcake and her

friends want to celebrate spring.

What can they do?

The girls have a berry good idea.

Let's have a Butterfly Parade!

The whole town can come.

Everyone will dress in springtime colors.

Our butterfly friends will lead

the way.

Flutter, flutter, flutter!

March, march, march!

Hooray for the parade!

Now Raspberry Torte has

a berry good idea.

She will make butterfly costumes

for her friends to wear.

She will sew fresh and fruity

dresses with long, glossy wings.

It will be a surprise!

Strawberry will be berry

pretty in red.

Lemon Meringue will look

lovely in yellow.

Blueberry Muffin will dazzle
in blue.

Plum Pudding will sparkle
in purple.

Orange Blossom will glimmer
in orange.

Cherry Jam will shimmer
in pink.

Raspberry is excited!

She stays up all night sewing.

One, two, three costumes done.

Four, five, six costumes finished.

Now it is time for Raspberry

to make her own costume.

Oh no! It is morning.

Raspberry will not have time

to make her costume.

She delivers the costumes

to her friends.

They are surprised and happy!

But they are sad when they see

Raspberry does not have

a costume.

What can the girls do?

They come up with a plan.

They send the butterflies

to find supplies.

The butterflies gather
spring flowers from all over
Berry Bitty City.

The girls make a crown

out of flowers.

Then they take a cape

and pin more flowers all over it.

They go to Raspberry's house.

Surprise, Raspberry!

We are crowning you

Queen of the Butterfly Parade!

You were a berry good friend
to make such beautiful costumes
for us.

We love them!

We love you, too!

Raspberry claps her hands.

She loves her new flower crown
and cape.

She hops on the back of

a butterfly.

It is time to start the parade!

Three cheers for spring!